Into the Tub

Written by Laura J. Beaver and Jill P. Nolen

Illustrated by Doug Pruett

Silver Ink Publishing

lisher's Cataloging-In-Publication Data (Prepared by The Donohue Group, Inc.)
aver, Laura J.
o the tub / written by Laura J. Beaver and Jill P. Nolen ;
rated by Doug Pruett ; edited by Kristin Reynolds.
v. (unpaged) : col. ill. ; 23 cm. + 1 guide.
BN: 0-9753113-5-2
edtime-- Juvenile fiction. 2. Mice-- Juvenile fiction. 3. Stories in rhyme.
eaders (Preschool) I. Nolen, Jill P. II. Pruett, Doug. III. Reynolds, Kristin. V. Title.

3.3.B438 Int 2004

As Sadie played with Sammy in the grass and the leaves,

she heard her mommy call, "Let's clean up now, please!"

CHIME TIME

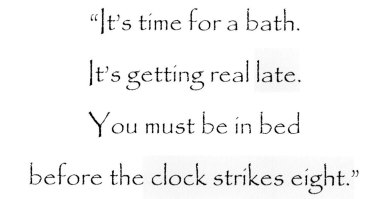

"It's time for a bath.

It's getting real late.

You must be in bed

before the clock strikes eight."

CHIME TIME

Sadie STOMPED!

Sadie squealed!

Sadie threw her toys around!

Then she plopped herself right down onto the ground.

"Now pick up your toys and do what Mommy said.

You have to take a bath. It's almost time for bed."

Into the tub...
boy, Sadie was mad.
"There, there, Sadie...
it's not so bad!

"Ten little fingers, ten little toes, two little ears, one shiny nose."

"Now to the shoulders, down to the knees..."

"Don't forget my belly!"

Sadie squealed with glee.

Splish, splish, splash... now Sadie wasn't sad.

Taking a bath was not so bad.

Cups,

soap,

ducks and boats,

sudsy bubbles and things that float!

"Now it's time to dry off.

It's getting real late.

You must be in bed

before the clock strikes eight."

CHIME TIME

Sadie whined.

Sadie pouted.

Sadie cried and cried.

"No, no, no! Why, Mommy, why?"

"Let's wipe away those tears
and do what Mommy said.
It's almost eight o'clock,
and you must go to bed."

CHIME TIME

Into the bed...boy, Sadie was mad.

"There, there, Sadie...it's not so bad!

Ten little fingers,

ten little toes,

two sleepy eyes

ready to close."

"Now for a story,
and for a song..."
"Don't forget my teddy!"
Sadie said with a yawn.

Into the Tub

Under the covers...now Sadie wasn't sad.
Going to bed was not so bad.

Pillow,
teddy,
story and song
bring sweet dreams that last all night long.

CHIME TIME

Mommy hugged Sadie
and kissed her sweet head.
She pulled up the covers
and tucked Sadie into bed.

Snug as a bug,
Sadie slept through the night.
Listening to Mommy
made things turn out right.

TELL IT AGAIN

StoryTime Activities

After reading a book aloud several times, choose at least one activity to do with your child from each category listed below.

- ■ About Books
- ■ About Reading
- ■ About Words
- ■ About Sounds
- ■ About Meaning

ABOUT BOOKS

Targets: Comprehension

Look at the front cover. Read aloud the title and the names of the author and illustrator. Tell your child that the author writes the words and the illustrator draws the pictures.

Show your child how to hold a book. As you turn the pages, talk about how a book is read: left to right and top to bottom.

Point out the parts of a book such as the front cover, title page, illustrations, words and punctuation.

Read different types of books. Read make-believe stories (fiction) and stories about real animals, people or things (nonfiction).

Read or sing nursery rhymes, short poems or songs.

ABOUT READING

Targets:
Fluency and Comprehension

Read the story with enthusiasm. Use facial expressions to make it more interesting.

Change your voice to match the characters in the story. Make your voice sound silly, scary, excited or angry to express the character's emotions.

Point to each word as you read the story. Children will learn that the words on the page tell the story and that you are not making them up.

Read your child's favorite books over and over.

Read books with rhyming words and books with words or phrases that repeat throughout the story.

Turn the page for more StoryTime Activities. ▶

StoryTime Activities

ABOUT WORDS

Targets: Vocabulary and Comprehension

Have your child act out words from the story that show feelings or actions. Examples: *stomped*, *squealed*, *whined*

Talk about the meaning of unfamiliar words or events from the story. Examples: *plop*, *glee*, *clock strikes eight*

Find a word that matches one of the pictures in the story. Point to the word, read it aloud and then let your child find the picture.

Use crayons, markers or magnet letters to display your child's name in your house. Help your child begin to recognize, spell and write his or her name.

ABOUT SOUNDS

Targets: Phonemic Awareness and Phonics

As you read the story talk about words that sound the same or rhyme. Example: Can you think of another word that sounds like *sad* and *bad*?

Label objects in your house that mean something to your child (bed, toy box, bookshelf, refrigerator, etc.). Write the words or print them from a computer and place each word on or near the object.